Balancing Act

Neil Moffatt

Balancing Act

This little novel will make you question some of the ways of the World you might take for granted. It starts as a series of apparently disconnected short chapters, each painting a small picture. The theme behind these vignettes is revealed in a revelation that grips the entire planet.

First edition published in June 2008
Second edition published in March 2011
This third edition published in December 2018

ISBN: 9781791594824

Feedback very welcome to ~~**fb@thinkmore.org.uk**~~
moffatt.neil
@gmail.com

Dora and Vince

Dora O'Hallaghan, the grey haired lady at the Ashram Convenience Store turned to get a half bottle of Vodka from the shelves of alcohol behind her. She did so slowly enough to give her slightly anxious customer just enough time to furtively take a bar of extra creamy Galaxy chocolate from the counter, and slide it into his pocket. Dora was a kindly lady, and would never have suspected an act of theft so brazen as this. She was completely oblivious to the heist, asking only for the money for the alcohol.

Outwardly calm, but inwardly beaming at his success, Vincent Axiom made a rapid exit from the shop, smuggling the illegally gained prize in his coat pocket. When far enough away from the shop, he unwrapped and bit into the chocolate. The creamy taste erupted into his mouth, enveloping him with a deliciously warm, relaxed feeling, submerging any thoughts of guilt.

But all was not quite right. In his haste to leave the store, only now did he realise that he had been short changed by the lady. He was in a good mind to go back and complain, but even he was just too aware of the hypocrisy of such an action.

Damn.

How could he have been so stupid.

Alas, things were to take one more bad turn that day. Or, more correctly, his stomach was to take a turn. Whilst the chocolate had left a nice taste in his mouth, it had not done the same to his stomach, and he retired to sleep curled up into the foetal position, with a bucket beside his bed. He felt awful, yet mindful

enough to wonder why buckets always seem to have that nauseating bleached smell.
He also wondered quite how a sublimely delicious bar of chocolate could have messed up his insides so much. Or maybe it had been the curry he had had for lunch?

Yea, that's it, the Hunjuraj Palace Tandoori Indian restaurant would no longer be receiving his custom, that is for sure. Oh no, daddy-oh, no! They would be certain to suffer a serious loss of income as a consequence!

Dora never noticed her monetary mistake.

Enid and Henry

Enid climbed the stairs to wake up her husband Henry. This couple were in their early 50's, still as much in love as in their courting days. She was relatively sprightly, but encumbered most of her days helping her husband who was heavily handicapped by rheumatoid arthritis. This condition swells the limbs, severely limiting movement, to the point where someone afflicted as much as Henry becomes housebound.

She knocked on the door.

"I've brought your breakfast up – you awake yet?" she asked.

"Yup" he replied.

When she entered the room, something was not quite right. Henry was sitting upright in the bed with a big smile on his face. Whilst this would be an ordinary matter for you and I, for Henry it was not.

"Thought I'd surprise you. I know it's hard for you to lift me up so I did it all on my own today." he explained.

Except that he had not done that for at least five years.

Enid was happy in a calm, gentle kind of way, preferring to enjoy this unexpected upturn in Henry's health rather than puzzle over its origin. However, Henry was undoubtedly happier – a small achievement like this was going to fuel an upbeat mood for the remainder of the day. Enid sat on the edge of the bed, and they talked with a lightened mood. Neither mentioned the strangeness of his newly acquired mobility for neither wanted to break the tranquility of the moment.

Vince and Tony

"Hiya Vince, how's it hanging?" Carl asked as the door swung open.

"Getting better – had a bad gut last night." Vince replied.

It was 9 o'clock the next day, and his slightly unsettling friend Carl had made a surprise visit.

"Couldn't have been the curry – remember, we had the same meal. Of course, if you can't handle Chicken Vindaloo ..."

"Nah, course I can. I thought at first that it was the chocolate I ate." Vince said, strangely feeling uncomfortable discussing stolen goods.

"What, chocolate poisoning? Only someone like Neil would get that!"

"You're right. Besides, the chocolate tasted OK. What you up to today?"

"I'm off to Grange Park to hang around with Joe and the others. Nothing special – wanna come along?"

They trundled off to become part of an assembly of young people called a gang. And it is a fact about gangs that they seem to have a compunction to assert themselves. To carry out acts of great daring in order to legitimise their status. So they decided, in their not so great wisdom, to steal a bicycle.

Now the bicycle they had their eye on was owned by Julian, a gangly youth, who was entirely incapable of defending himself against such a theft. Minutes later, swiftly removed from ownership of his bright red bicycle, Julian could only watch as it sped away. It was Tony, the most bullish member of the gang, who had carried out the broad daylight theft.

He sped away with an evil roar in his throat, past the tennis courts, and stupidly straight into one of the rarest sights you can behold in modern Britain – a policeman on his beat.

The poor constable suffered a bruised shin, but Tony landed so awkwardly that he dislocated his shoulder. And his ego.

Like a puff of smoke, the gang disbanded, swiftly dissolving into the distance, leaving Tony to face the music. The speed of their retreat benefited from the absence of even the slightest sense of loyalty to the now stranded Tony.

Poor Tony was helped to his feet by the policeman. Not without some shrieks of pain, however, as the policeman had chosen his injured arm to try to lift him up.

The two of them stood there, vociferously informing the small group of onlookers that they ached. As the policeman and Tony groaned and grimaced, Julian gained the confidence to recover his stolen bicycle.

"He nicked my bike!" Julian exclaimed to the policeman.

To which, the policeman asked Tony if this were indeed true.

"It was only a joke – I was just having a little ride and was going to give it right back. Honest I was." he said in his defence.

"Liar - you sneered when you took it." Julian riposted.

Fortunately for Julian, the policeman had indeed witnessed enough of the event to see what had actually happened, so proceeded to accompany Julian home, along with an obviously reluctant Tony. You see, it just happened that this policeman was not bothered by the formalities of his profession, that should have seen him now filling in copious numbers of forms. Instead, he felt the best way to treat the villainous boy was for him to meet the parents of his victim.

This was painful indeed for Tony, for he now had to bear the wrath of Julian's somewhat intimidating father Brian. Rather than punish Tony on the spot, Brian followed the lead of the policeman, and elected to take Tony home to discuss the matter with Tony's parents. When they arrived, Tony's father, George, was asked on the spot to pay a reasonable sum for damages. He was numbed into doing so by the presence of the policeman.

After Brian and the policeman had departed, a sullen looking Tony was left alone with his stern father, who explained that he would have to pay the full amount of the bike damages out of his weekly allowance.

As if this were not enough, Tony received a cuff around the ear that left it pink and throbbing.

So Tony felt doubly aggrieved of course. And puzzled also, for he had no idea why he had earlier been unable to avoid cycling straight at the policeman. It was as if he was being pushed inexorably towards his fate.

By contrast, Julian decided that life was not so tough after all, his finances now unexpectedly supplemented by the damages payment.

Sarah

Allegiances in Sarah Troutman's class were clearly divided between the Chelsea, Manchester United, Liverpool and Arsenal fans and the real football fans. Whilst Sarah saw herself as a true blue Chelsea fan, if truth be told, she was swayed more by their recent success than any affinity with football in that particular part of London.

What set her aside from her cohorts, however, was her deeply held Christian beliefs.

So it was pretty inevitable that one day she would be found kneeling down, praying to God for Chelsea to win one more match, and thereby regain the Premiership title from their fierce rivals, Manchester United.

She prayed :

"You know how good I try to be God. I only normally pray for the good fortune of others, so can I ask just once for something for myself?

Actually, it is not even for me – it is for my football team. They really, really want to win the league. Manchester United have won it so many times, it must be time that Chelsea won again.

Please, please, I'll go to church more often. Just this one request"

"Thank you Lord for listening to my prayer."

Both Chelsea and Manchester United lost on the last day of the season, allowing Liverpool to win the league for the first time in decades. Sarah was none too pleased.

Matthew

Matthew Bradman worked in Japan, monitoring seismic activity on the island of Honshu, underneath which the Eurasian and Pacific tectonic plates overlap.

He was principally employed to look for trends in the behaviour of these indescribably large lumps of matter, trying as best as he could to predict any possible volcanic or earthquake activity that can result from the abrasion of the plates with each other.

These huge plates are essentially a law unto themselves, choosing almost arbitrarily when to jostle their shoulders against each other, often giving false alarms. If you evacuate a city when nothing ensues then you're in big trouble. However, we've all seen what happens when an earthquake happens with no prior warning.

However, Matthew was noticing a new pattern of tectonic behaviour. It was unlike any he had seen in his twelve years in the job. The inter-plate noise was actually gradually reducing.

This sounded like good news of course, but his experience told him otherwise. This might instead mean the lull before the storm, much like the suddenly, unexpected receding waters on a beach that signal the imminent arrival of a tsunami.

So he went to amber alert, and cancelled his upcoming holiday. You see, Matthew was very dedicated to his job, and was somewhat worried about the possible ramifications of this new discovery. He had to be extra vigilant in the days and weeks ahead, and could not enjoy a holiday in such circumstances.

Seagulls

"Why is it that we can never find anywhere to park? The council are forever restricting roads to residents only. They complain about the big out of town supermarkets, but we cannot use the local shops because we just cannot park"

Phyllis said all this in frustration to little George, her 8 year old grandson, not for his benefit but simply because someone had to hear what she wanted to say.

"Ah, here we go, at last!" she said as she homed in on a gap in a row of parked cars.

That she straddled both a double yellow line and the zigzag that preceded a pedestrian crossing clearly did not register in her mind. With the target of parking achieved, off she strode, poor George's little legs struggling to keep up with her.

She knew that it was safe of course to infringe parking regulations like this, because council cutbacks had made traffic wardens an almost invisible breed.

However, Phyllis' car was bright red, precisely the colour that most readily caught the attention of a flockette of three sharp-eyed seagulls with some excess baggage to unload.

Whoosh, and Phyllis' car was now pebble dashed. The seagulls were proud of their accuracy, and would have smiled if their beaks had let them.

Smiling, however, was not the first thought that sprung to her mind when Phyllis returned to her now multi coloured Mini Coupe.

Ginger

It was very dark now, and therefore a good time to scout along the lane that lay between Alberta Terrace and Calgary Drive. The rear gardens were unusually equipped with low privet hedges rather than high fences or walls, affording Dave 'Ginger' Roberts full view of the rear of each house. He needed his torch light, however, as the lane had no lighting.

He saw a house without lights, extending to an outhouse with a flat roof. That would do. He checked both ways to make sure that he was alone, and then eased the back gate latch open, making sure it shut quietly behind him.

He tiptoed along the path, with that heightened sense of awareness that the seasoned criminal develops. He was vigilant like a cat approaching its prey, not wishing to make its presence known.

As he had hoped, the top-right bedroom window was slightly ajar – an open invitation that he believed entirely legitimised his planned intrusion. If they're going to make it easy for you to get in, then they'll learn a hard lesson. You see, even burglars have to justify what they do to themselves.

Still in cat mode, he climbed onto the bin, up onto the flat roof, along in a crouch, ever so carefully easing the window open before slipping inside. He had checked first that the room was empty.

Mr and Mrs Summers were out enjoying themselves. They had left the hall light on, but this was not visible from the rear. He had entered their son's room, and moved quickly downstairs to the lounge. He had a 35 litre rucksack, enough for a tasty iPad or X-Box. The LED TV was tempting, but just too big.

He scanned the room, then shuffled through the drawers of the display cabinet. Much to his surprise, he found a jewellery box and a wallet.

His luck was in.

He tipped the box contents into the lower section of his rucksack, and zipped it tight. He rifled through the wallet, extracting around £120 in five and ten pound notes into his pocket. As he dropped the wallet, three photographs slipped out of the middle, windowed section. They landed onto the table face-up.

Underneath the TV was a Blu-Ray player. This was indeed a very lucky strike. A good day.

You have to remember that these things were not for himself. Any burglar of reasonable experience had all the electronic equipment he needed. He would sell his ill-gotten gain at the car boot sale on Sunday morning, and be set up for a week of beer and the odd spliff.

As he untangled the wires from the Sony Blu-Ray player, he kept his ears open for any tell-tale sign of humans. And that also meant other burglars.

After slipping the player into the main part of his rucksack, he scanned the kitchen before returning to the lounge on his way back upstairs. As he passed through the lounge, his eye caught the upended wallet on the table. He sat down and looked at the photos. Obviously, the couple not only had a good camera, which he had yet to find, but also very pretty children.

One photo was of the family. All were beaming except the husband, who looked somewhat sad. He wondered why they kept that particular photo. Maybe it was the only one taken on that day, and the memory of the day was more important than his downbeat appearance.

It was not like Ginger to linger.

Here he was, in the middle of a burglary, and he was looking over family belongings. Not only that, but he was getting deeply distracted, trying to work out why the husband was sad.

He tried to picture this man when he arrived home later that night. That sad expression came to his mind. Poor bugger, he thought to himself!

"Don't get soft now, Ginge" he said to himself.

But having felt a change of mindset, he saw for the first time what he was doing. No, not the stealing itself. But what the stealing did to people. They would come home and feel more than their losses. They would feel abused. How could he not have seen this before? What was going on? Why was he doing this?

He ripped open the rucksack, and tipped the Sony player out onto the sofa. He removed the jewels from the zipped compartment, placing them next to the player. He withdrew the notes from his pocket, and placed them next to the jewellery box. He returned to the kitchen, and scribbled on the wipe clean board that he was sorry for invading their house.

He felt genuinely sorry that he had no time to leave tidily.

He sped upstairs, through the window, onto the roof and down into the garden, leaving as quietly as he had arrived, but otherwise quite a different person.

As he started walking home, his head bowed low, he decided to check how many houses along the road he was. He then marched that same number along the house fronts so that he could find out the number of the house he had infiltrated.

You see, later that day, he would write a letter to Mr and Mrs Summers, even though his letter would not be addressed to them by name of course. They were an anonymous target of his petty theft, and he was now able to see such theft for what it was. He felt a strange mix of emotions, having already decided to go on the straight and narrow. He was going to have to find some other way of paying for his vices, which was a pain, but writing the letter would end this sordid time of his life.

He felt sweetly elevated in mood by his new enlightenment.

Leonard

Some car repair garages have unenviable, but justified reputations for cowboy repairs, and Thomson's Auto Repairs was no exception. So it was well within their capabilities to overlook minor, trivial details, like, you know, a hand brake that was teetering on the edge of failure.

Which is exactly why Leonard Smith should never have parked his car on a hill. Indeed, this was a very bad idea. Some minutes after he had left the car to go shopping, the very blustery conditions in combination with the rush of a monster Tesco lorry was just enough to ease his car into an irreversible downward descent. Ever so slowly at first, as the hand brake hung in there, gallantly trying to carry out its simple role to the very end. But the car was soon out of control, the handbrake now ineffective. It headed unmanned towards the busy shopping street below, and a morass of unsuspecting shoppers.

It careered towards a line of pedestrians at a bus stop along the way, but somehow managed to stay on track on the road. A few gave it puzzled looks, wondering exactly what the driver was doing, completely out of sight. By the time the road started levelling out, the car had picked up a fair speed, with the handbrake now useless in stopping its advance.

Thora Jones was 90, and had an unfortunate habit of stepping onto zebra crossings without checking that vehicles had noticed her. She ambled ever so slowly across, assuming in all her innocence that cars should stop as a matter of course. And yes, normally they did. But now we are talking about a car without a conscience, speeding straight towards the oblivious old lady.

Witnesses said afterwards that they could hear the squeal of brakes as the car abruptly came to a halt precisely at the edge of the zebra crossing. And that Thora remained unaware of her very lucky escape. The Police were called, but dismissed all witnesses as unreliable. They towed the car away, and contacted the Swansea DVLA to inform the driver of the whereabouts of his vehicle.

When Leonard returned later that day to go home in his car, he was somewhat disappointed to find that it had been 'nicked'. When he later recovered the car, no explanation was provided as to what had happened to it.

So Leonard was left very puzzled and worse off to the sum of £125, the fee to reclaim his vehicle.

Enid and Henry again

What started out as a little game each morning gradually progressed, as Henry slowly regained feeling and mobility in his limbs. The swelling reduced, and he was able to make his own way downstairs, revelling in the delight of afternoons relaxing in the garden as Enid pottered around weeding and planting flowers and shrubs.

Whilst Enid was delighted in this strange change of events, she still felt that Henry should seek a medical opinion to try to explain his health reversal. Henry was reluctant because he believed that his positive outlook was influencing his condition, and that Doctor Jones was never very sympathetic with his plight at the best of times.

But Enid won her way and a series of tests were carried out on Henry. The results duly baffled the medical profession. Degenerative conditions did not reverse as seamlessly as they appeared to be doing in Henry's case.

Had he been taking any additional supplements they asked? Taking more exercise than normal? They insisted that he must have been doing something to reverse this situation.

And for once, they did indeed hear his tales of positive thinking.

The "Power of the mind" he told them.

But they only listened so as to humour him, and recorded a verdict yet again of "Spontaneous remission" in their notes without ever stopping to wonder what was really going on. They were medics – they only worked on things that were wrong with people. When their patients got better, they were no longer interested, which was a profoundly sad attitude of course, denying them the opportunity to learn about good health.

One day, rather a long time in the future, they would learn to realise that investigations into "spontaneous healings" would open the door to new realms of healing knowledge.

Catherine and Charlie

British comedy rarely survives the trans-Atlantic journey to the United States of America mostly because it so often portrays its cast as self-effacing. With their euphoric, upbeat focus on individual achievement, to lampoon yourself if you are American is just not funny.

This British habit extends to the alternative naming of institutions. So it is that the 'Crown and Sceptre' pub, tucked away in a side street behind Upper Regent Street in Central London is better known by Catherine Blobby and her cohorts as the 'Hat and Stick'.

In addition to her unfortunate name, poor Catherine also had to suffer the somewhat more tangible fates of being pig-ugly, and as thick as two planks. Two very short but substantial planks. Not only that, she was also blessed with a naturally tactless nature. A diplomat she was not!

We find her today in dialogue with her best friend Charlie, a very tolerant, understanding lady, herself beset with certain 'problems', probably best not delved into here.

"I noticed it on Monday last week," Catherine said to Charlie.

"I've checked loads of photos and my jaw is *definitely* not so long."

"What the hell are you on about, Cath? We meet for the first time in over a week and you start talking rubbish again" Charlie replied.

"Sorry Charlie, but you've got to believe me – just look. Look now – see how my face is rounder."
Charlie scrutinised Catherine's face and was not convinced. Part of the reason is that people in general are not terribly observant. They delude themselves into thinking they are, but they miss much more than they would like to think they do.

Catherine rummaged into her bag and lifted out an envelope containing two photographs of herself. Although not taken at the same angle, it was evident to the layman that her face had changed shape. But faces do not change shape just like that. Well, not as quickly as this without surgery.

Which explained Charlie's incredulity. She gazed at these photos, but her mind kept drifting off.

"And," Catherine continued, "men look at me more often".

But Charlie was not really listening. One of the reasons she was able to be tolerant with Catherine was that she frequently drifted away into a different world, oblivious to whatever Catherine was talking about.

They upped and left, Catherine irritated by Charlie's indifference. As they departed, Catherine's eye caught that of a young man who had just entered. The visual embrace lasted a few seconds before the man held the door open for them.

"What was that all about?" Charlie asked Cath when out of earshot.

"OK, maybe *now* you understand what I am on about! I look different, and men are starting to notice. Oh, and I've started reading books as well."

"You never read books. You've always said you hated them."

"No idea why, but I can kinda understand them better now" Catherine ventured, as she ambled along the road.

Charlie walked alongside her wondering what on earth was going on in the mind of her friend. This just might be one crazy thing too many for her to cope with.

Sarah again

A week after the end of the football season, Sarah was to be found with tears rolling down both of her cheeks. The television programme she was watching was covering the devastation wreaked on an African village by the continuing drought conditions. No rain had fallen in fully eight months and all but one of the water wells had dried up.

The sheer reality of the situation was made graphic by the televisual imagery, but Sarah barely needed that. From her privileged position of comfort in Britain, she was very aware of the plight of the villagers. And the only thing she felt she could do to help now was to pray for rain for them. She knelt down by her bed, and spoke rather than thought her prayer :

"Dear God, the situation in Africa is very bad now. Please, please can you help the rains fall so that the people don't die a miserable death? Please God hear my prayer. Amen."

She paused, head bowed, hoping that this respect would give her prayer an extra sense of power.

As she was about to stand up, the room went very, very quiet. She paused, sitting on the end of her bed. She heard no sound of cars, of birdsong. Gone was the tinkle of trees rustling. She could not say for sure if she could even hear the sound of her own heart. But it was not a cold, oppressive quiet. It had a gentle calmness.

Until, that is, she heard a voice speak.

Thank you Sarah.

The situation is in hand – I will help them shortly.

She looked around and could see no one.

"Who was that? You're frightening me."

Please do not fear.

You will learn more soon.

This is all I can say now.

Sarah asked if she was hearing the voice of God, but the voice was no longer to be heard. Instead, the calm quiet disappeared as fast as it had arrived.

She ran from her room, raced down the stairs, and jogged to the All Saints Methodist Church a couple of streets away. It was a Wednesday afternoon, but there was a chance that the Vicar would be there. She had to tell someone that she had heard the voice of God. At least, this is what she hoped she had heard.

She was in luck, finding Reverend John Vectis preparing a sermon for the upcoming Sunday. She approached him with an explosion of words that she of course had to repeat at a measured pace. John was not a man to be rushed. Oh no.

However, he was a good listener, waiting until the end of the second run of her monologue before speaking.

"This is what happened, my child?" he asked.

"Yes, of course" she replied.

"Have you been studying hard for your exams? Maybe you are starting to hear things?"

"You don't believe me, do you? I guessed you wouldn't."

"But what you are saying is very profound. You know this."

They spoke further but never in accord. You see, it is not possible for the ego of even a humble, deeply religious man such as John to countenance the possibility that someone else would be spoken to directly by God. He himself had received guidance from the almighty, but always via mere signs and other subtle means. He always had to interpret God's meanings in the things that happened around him.

He felt short-changed that here was this young lady claiming to have been chosen to hear His voice in all its glory. This was not right – if God was going to speak, then surely only one of the most devoutly religious of his flock should be the blessed recipient.

He hastened to clear his mind of these selfish thoughts, and humoured Sarah, in as kind a manner as he could muster in the circumstances, allowing her to hold onto the dream that she had been the chosen one. Yes, that's right, this would help her grow into a fine upstanding Christian woman.

Sarah bought his words readily, allowing herself to feel so special that she floated on air for days.

Greg

Gregory Julian Roberts was known by friends as Greg, and by his enemies as Caveman, probably because of his somewhat primitive appearance and behaviour. And he was known by his younger sister Emily as the Evil Bully.

His view, as the eldest child, was that he had to keep Emily in check. She, of course, did not share this view. Naturally, she hated the way that he treated her with disdain and contempt.

On this particular day, Greg had endured a very annoying time at school that had included a double Maths lesson. To Greg, Mathematics was a form of torture that he never grasped. So Emily became the inevitable outlet for him to let off steam.

"Gimme some of your chocolate" he ordered his sister.

"No – get yer own." she defiantly replied.

He tried to grab it, but she was too fast. So brute force was needed. He grabbed her arm and twisted it behind her back. The half eaten chocolate bar dropped to the floor. He grabbed it and pinched her leg for good measure.

As he did so, he felt her pinch his leg.

"You cheeky fing, pinching back. Fink you're tough?"

"What cho on about, I didn't touch ya" she replied.

He pinched her again, and felt her pinch him back. Except that he could now see that her arms were indeed not moving. He

slapped her leg smartly, and felt a smack on his leg at exactly the same time.
"You got some special powers now or sumfink?" he asked her.

"What cho on abou'. I ain't done nufink." she exclaimed.

Being somewhat retarded of mind, it took rather a lot of attacks on poor Emily before Greg realised that whatever he did to her happened back to him with equal measure. But when the penny eventually did drop, he left her alone.

For the next few days, he warily kept a comfortable distance. When Emily realised that she was no longer likely to be arbitrarily bullied, her attitude to Greg lightened up.

She stopped teasing him, and felt a resurgence of sisterly love. This in turn had a reciprocal effect on Greg, and over the coming weeks, they started warming to each other.

Whether it was this closer bonding, or a lingering fear about that strange day, Greg never hurt her again.

John

Two days later, John Vectis was sitting comfortably at home watching the television. And for once, some good news lightened the fare – a monsoon was bringing much welcome relief to large parts of Western Africa. The BBC had commentary from the same village they reported on two days ago. The dusty scene of drought shown then was now replaced by an altogether different one, where children were dancing bare-foot in the rain.

It took a few moments for John to be nudged by this news into remembering what Sarah had said to him in great excitement on Wednesday. Could this really be the same village she had been talking about? Instinctively, he realised that this was indeed the most likely reality, and a deep feeling started brewing in the pit of his stomach.

Is it really possible that God would speak to someone like Sarah, and then carry out her prayer? We are all equal in the eyes of the Lord, but surely he and the countless other religious dignitaries around the World were better recipients of His almighty attention?

He had to contact her.

Fortunately, details of all the regulars at the church were held in the office, and he headed that way in all haste, swiftly finding Sarah's telephone number.

"This is Reverend John here. Is that Sarah?" he asked into his mobile phone.

"Hi John. That's very flattering, but no, it's her Mother. She's out at the moment. Was there anything special that I can help you with?" Megan replied.

"Thanks, but I really do need to speak to Sarah personally. When will she be back?"

"Actually, not that long. But you might want to ring her on her mobile since she passes the church on her way home."

Megan gave him Sarah's mobile number, and he immediately rang her. She agreed to meet with him, in maybe 20 minutes time, at the church. When she arrived, the roles now reversed, and it was his turn to be the energised, excited one. He explained about the monsoons, and as he did so, a serene, sweet smile slowly lit Sarah's face, giving her an angelic look.

For a while, they both sat there, allowing the impact of what they shared to start to fully dawn upon them.

"I'll take you home Sarah. Thank you so much for dropping by. I think you realise the importance of all this, and I trust that we can keep it to ourselves for the time being. Is that OK?" he said.

"Yes, yes, of course. Besides, I'm not sure anyone would actually believe me anyway" she replied, as she slipped out of the church.

"Do you want me to escort you home?" John asked as she left.

"No, but thanks anyway."

When the last person had left the church, John sat in the rearmost pew, too humble to take a more advanced position, and prayed like he had not prayed before. He hoped, desperately hoped, that God would also talk to him.

But no quiet descended upon him. No tranquil voice entered his head.

Hospital

The Oncology Department of Birmingham Children's Hospital is necessarily a very sad place to the eyes of most visitors. Seeing someone afflicted by the latter stages of cancer is hard for anyone to take in. To see this in a young person magnifies this feeling enormously.

But today, Doctor Michael Brown entered the ward with a sprightly spring to his step. And an irresistible smile that his professionalism was unable to hide.

They had checked the scans of all eleven children in the ward. Checked again and again until there was no doubt.

"Hello Hannah, how are you feeling today?" he asked the 7 year old girl in the first bed.

"Hello Doctor Brown. I'm alright." she replied

"Do you miss being at home?"

"Of course I do. My bed is much nicer than this one."

"Do you want to go home then?"

"Can I? Am I better? Who is going to take me home?"

Doctor Brown left her side for a moment to usher in her parents. He had spoken to them earlier. They swung the curtain around little Hannah, allowing her parents some privacy to dress her. You could hear Hannah being hugged, and the soft whimpering sound of her Mother as she all but squeezed the life out of her only child.

Doctor Brown moved to the next child, and announced to her also that she may go home. But before he moved to the third bed, he noticed the anxious eyes of the nine other children were bearing down on him. This was not going to be so easy, he realised. He was going to have to break protocol, and make an announcement to all the children.

"You are all going to go home today. Your parents are outside waiting. You are all free from cancer. We do not understand why, but please just go home and enjoy your lives – you have all been wonderfully well-behaved patients."

He told Nurse Dickens to bring the parents in.

He left as they arrived, unable to cope with the surge in energy that permeated the ward.

Parents and children laughed and cried, emotions all mixed up.

Matthew again

"Bharami, did you get the trace file?" Matthew asked his Indian colleague by telephone.

"Yes I did," he replied "and normally I would understand your concern. But the trace signature does not follow any patterns I've seen before."

Bharami was one of a number of seismology contacts Matthew regularly used. Seismic behaviour was often best understood via the bigger picture – collating the pockets of information from around the World often furnished greater understanding of local behaviour.

"The trace is not just quiet, which can be worrying – it is actually declining – it is getting quieter. The seismic activity is diminishing. You can trust my confidence in this judgement because I too have recorded the same pattern in the Indian Ocean" Bharami said.

"We need to arrange a conference as soon as we can to get a grip on this. To say that this is an exciting development is something of an understatement. Are you available next week to meet up in Japan? I've been in contact with Horato in Kyoto and he tells the same story." Matthew replied.

"I'm busy until Thursday, but can free up the weekend if that's OK."

This was the first of a number of phone calls that helped coordinate the first emergency seismic conference since the 1995 Kyoto earthquake. Matthew thought it appropriate to meet at the epicentre of that quake.

Enid and Henry yet again

It was Enid's 53rd birthday party. As always, she anticipated a quiet day, and a big hug and kiss in lieu of a present from her housebound husband.

But this year was different. Henry had acquired so much mobility now that he had started meeting up at the allotment with his friends twice a week. Or at least this is what Enid had been led to believe. But Henry had split his allotted time, so to speak, in two. One day chatting at the allotment with his gardener friends, and the other working part time in a garden centre.

So he had earned enough money to be able to surprise Enid with a second hand sewing machine as a birthday present, one of those clever ones that can even embroider your name.

He had to explain, of course, that he had, well, sort of lied to her about his part time job.

"Oh Henry, why did you go and do such a thing for me? You big old softy!" she exclaimed.

"After all you've done for me, it was the very least I could have done as a small thanks" he replied.

"But I have another surprise for you as well. Gretchins, the garden centre, are going to let me work five afternoons a week, starting next month" he continued, and then had to placate Enid, who tried to insist that he take it easy instead.

You see, Henry was not lazy by nature, and had felt imprisoned by his crippling arthritis. He was a new man now, like a boy with his first pay-slip. And he wanted to live life to the full. If it meant a bit of discomfort from hard work, then so be it.

Not so many weeks later Enid also decided to return to work. Their joint incomes eventually earned them enough money to buy a caravan and set off on a tour of the Cotswold's and the Lake District. And, some months later still, they were able to fly to Canada to visit their daughter's family.

Geoffrey and Ben

Geoffrey Forde was a frustrated man. Having finally acquired all the acres of fertile land he had aspired to, his body was no longer able to manage them. He could plant seeds and tend to them, but the digging required a garden assistant. And yet another had just let him down.

So it was that he started walking to the shops in a sour mood, not least because it was terribly windy. His compromised body struggled in such conditions.

As he arrived at the junction of Peter Street and Chilcott Terrace, steering his body towards the former, a series of wind gusts kept pushing him towards the latter. He could get to the shops that way, but it was a longer journey. He tried to fight the wind, but finally had to concede and set off on the path less travelled.

His day of frustrations was not quite over. After a hundred yards, a tremendously powerful gust finally threw him off his feet. He stumbled forward towards Ben, a sharp-minded homeless man who had been watching Geoffrey's perilous advance. He sprung to his feet and broke the fall of Geoffrey with great aplomb. It made him feel good for the first time this day, of value rather than a social eye-sore many sadly see him as.

When Geoffrey realised what had happened, he was terribly grateful to Ben.

"Thank you so much. You saved me serious injury I feel."

"No problem" Ben replied "happy to be in the right place and time."
Geoffrey was now quite obviously aware of Ben strength, and had the insight to realise that he could be of great value employed doing the heavy digging work on his allotments. And Ben was of course delighted to accept the offer, happy to be engaged in something meaningful, rather than a precarious pseudo-existence.

"You can sleep in the shed. It has a small night heater to keep it warm"

Both Ben and Geoffrey departed with raised spirits.

Locusts

Whilst Africa has historically been the most affected by infestations of pests, nearby Yemen had recently been bombarded by swarms of locusts that razed millet, rice and maize crops to the ground. Being relatively new to this form of attack, the impact had been devastating to the Yemen people, with many families crippled by malnutrition.

The effectiveness of pesticides had reduced in the last few years, with new breeds of locusts blatantly disregarding the rules and failing to die.

But this year, the crops were robust, and the expected locusts simply did not turn up. Maybe they had seen tastier fare elsewhere, but that seemed most unlikely. Or maybe the anti-locust tribal dances were being particularly efficacious for once.

The locals, were, let us say, cautiously ecstatic. And somewhat plumper than you would normally find them. Which is to say that they almost looked healthy.

The governments of the World were of course very much aware of unusual events like this, and were keeping a close eye on matters. They were looking for a common theme, as this was not an isolated incident, but they only had conjectures so far.

Dr Rowan Williams

Dr Rowan Williams, the Archbishop of Canterbury and head of the Church of England, had extensive responsibilities that were of course not confined to the shores of Great Britain. Sometimes, this weighed heavily on his shoulders.

Fortunately, apart from the occasional ill-judged comment, the head on these shoulders was a wise one.

On this particular day, which would be unlike any day before in his illustrious career, he was to be found researching material for a forthcoming Diocesan Conference in Hereford. He sat alone at his computer, having for some time taken advantage of modern technology to simplify his work.

He looked out of the window, pondering the plight of the homeless, and noticed a slight cool descend over the room. It was accompanied by a gentle quiet, as the sound of birds outside faded into the background.

He slowly released himself from his train of thought to embrace this inexplicable calm. His mind was clear, free from chatter and emotions.

The calm was softly broken by a strong but smooth voice.

Good evening Rowan.

The same voice that had spoken to Sarah some days ago now.

Being of passive disposition, Rowan did not react to the voice, a voice that sounded from within his head. He was relaxed and

receptive, and replied as if from Buddhist training in like fashion.
"I am fine. How are you?" he said, his eyes fixed upon the window, content to remain there, feeling no urgency to find the body that must surely accompany the voice.

I am fine.

Thank you for asking.

Rowan could sense something ethereal about the voice, something transcendental that was not really of this World. So he felt compelled to ask :

"Are you God?"

To which the voice replied :

Yes, that is the name by which you know me.

With the air still cool and calm, quiet and serene, Rowan sat and pondered this. He had been a key figure in various roles for his Church for many years now. The depth of his Christian faith was profound and unwavering.

But now he was apparently being spoken to by God with a clarity that mocked what he thought he had heard before. He was personally hearing the voice of the Almighty. And his heart was starting to race.

Minutes passed with no sound apart from the faster inhalation and exhalation of his breath.

"What do you want me to do, O Lord?" he eventually asked.

I ask of you a strange favour. I apologise that I do so this first time that we converse. I would like you to make arrangements with the British Broadcasting Corporation in London to present a television programme for International transmission. The programme will be of ten minutes duration, to take place after the last scheduled discussion at the Group of 8 Summit in Geneva next month. It is my hope that you are sufficiently well respected by the BBC for them to approve such a programme.

You must tell the BBC that the programme will be of significant International interest, but the content must remain confidential until the very time of the transmission itself.

You will have rightly guessed that I will be present for this broadcast, but I cannot say more now about the nature of the content. I ask that you keep my attendance a complete secret from the BBC, your friends and even your family.

Rowan sat a while to absorb this request.

"O Lord, please let me ask you one question. What you request I will surely do. I would travel to the ends of the World for you. But to hear your voice for the first time, and to hear such a request just seems extremely odd. It is surely too demeaning that you should be asking me to help you.

Can you enlighten me, just a little?" Rowan pleaded.

You are a fine man Rowan, and you have said many times that God works in mysterious ways. For now, I would like this purported habit of mine to be sustained just a little longer.

Rowan confirmed that he would make the arrangements, for which he was thanked, and then left alone in deep contemplation.

He had a lot to think about.

Mark Thompson

"Can I please speak to Mark Thompson. I am the Archbishop of Canterbury" Rowan asked the BBC switchboard. For the second time.

The first time that he had been connected through, the switchboard operator replied that he himself was the Duke of Kent, and put the phone down in a fit of giggles.

"Putting you through now, sir" the operator said this time.

Mark Thompson was about as busy a man as Rowan, albeit with a schedule that was somewhat different. He did, however, tend to field calls from dignitaries, risking the odd prank call.

"Good morning Rowan, this is a pleasant surprise. How can I help you?" Mark proffered.

"Good day to you, sir. And may I take the opportunity of thanking you for a splendid range of programmes, still the best broadcaster in the World" Rowan replied, always preferring to flatter as a gentle way into dialogue with powerful men.

"I have a difficult request of you I am afraid. I would ask, no, implore, that you are able to schedule a ten minute programme for an important international announcement I would like to make. It must be held in Geneva, Switzerland in July as the last item on the agenda of the G8 summit."

"This is somewhat unusual, you do realise, Rowan. Can you give me a flavour of the message you need to give?"

"Actually, I cannot. I really am in no position to release any details whatsoever prior to transmission. I can only offer you two things ...

... First that you will absolutely not regret the decision to proceed with the programme. And secondly, that as head of the Church of England, you can trust that my intentions are entirely honourable."

The line went quiet for a few moments.

"Excuse me a moment Rowan, I need to talk with the head of programmes. Can I call you back, or will you hold the line?" Mark asked.

"I'll hold. Please do not rush your decision. I understand that my request requires some thought."

But Mark did indeed agree to air this mystery programme, on the condition that the BBC had full marketing rights, and would be accredited as the producers. And of course it would be subject to approval from the organisers of the G8 summit. Not exactly an easy task, but Rowan had good powers of persuasion, and, most importantly, good contacts, so would readily be able to gain this approval.

Rowan accepted Mark's terms, and resumed his more traditional role as Religious leader rather than programme organiser. He heard no further word from God that day. He thought to tell God in a prayer exactly when the programme was due to go on air, but he assumed, quite rightly, that God would be fully aware of such matters.

Summit else

The position of Archbishop of Canterbury brought with it a great deal of international influence, and Rowan Williams was shrewd and open-minded enough to use this power to international benefit more than for elevating his own status.

So it was that the assembly of leading players in the Group of 8 most powerful countries at the Geneva summit was now supplemented by a strong representation of the leading figures of the World's diverse religions. Amazingly, this even included the Pope.

Most impressive, though, was how Rowan was able to attract these otherwise very busy figures without being able to tell them exactly what they would be witnessing or partaking in. Suffice to say, though, that his head was on the line if their mass attendance proved a disappointment.

The G8 representatives from the UK, USA, Canada, France, Germany, Japan, Italy and Russia were meeting for their annual 3 days of discussions on mutual and global matters, such as the environment, and the ever increasing divide between the wealthy nations and the so called 'Third World' nations.

These meetings regularly attracted heated protests, often simply because the actions agreed in many summits were mostly token, aimed more at deflecting criticism than in truly tackling the real problems that beset all but the G8 countries themselves.

The Geneva summit was much like those that preceded it, with the sympathy lavished on matters such as the perennial problem of AIDS in Africa rarely matched by tangible, meaningful promises. Always, the financial security of the G8 economies was carefully protected as a priority.

But this time, there were rumours circulating the activists sprinkled around the building in Geneva that something big was going to happen this year. The rumours were inconsistent, but widespread. Something special was indeed going to happen.

As the summit drew to an end on the third day, the atmosphere inside the building started reflecting that mood outside. The G8 representatives, the religious leaders and the audience were all increasingly wary that the final item on the agenda was the Summit summit, as it were – the pinnacle of the meeting – the icing on the cake.

The official line was for that a very special announcement would be made by an extra special guest. No details beyond this were provided, not even to the G8 reps.

The time eventually arrived, with the last discussion swiftly brought to an unusually premature close. The main lights faded out, leaving the whole building in near darkness, save for a few safety lights. A calm descended over all that were present.

The BBC cameras had started broadcasting, not really knowing what to expect.

A deep but gentle voice began to speak.

From this point onwards, the World would become a much different place.

The World listens

The voice spoke to those present and those Worldwide receiving the broadcast.

Good evening to you all. I am known to you most commonly by the name of God, or Allah.

A swell of emotion filled the room, but everyone remained remarkably quiet, transfixed by what they were hearing.

I must first apologise for taking this unusual measure to talk with you, my creatures. And I must also apologise for speaking in English. I believe that this is the most appropriate language for International broadcast.

I use the medium of television for very practical reasons. To communicate with all of you individually would take me far too long in my present condition.

As God spoke, the audience in the building remained transfixed in quiet shock. Those watching on televisions were reacting somewhat differently. Equally transfixed, but somewhat more noisily so.

I will first try to reassure you that I am who I say I am.

Such is the power of illusion in modern television, I am once again obliged to apologise – for the mechanism of this proof. Please bear with me, and please remain calm – no one will come to harm in what follows.

One by one, the G8 representatives slowly rose into the air to a height of about ten feet. The look on their faces was priceless, but they heeded God's word and remained composed.
At least mostly composed.

Please walk to the rear of the building.

Everyone had seen levitations on television, with raised figures sweeping across a stage. But no one had any doubt that these men walked as if on solid ground, tentatively at first, but with confidence gained, robustly striding towards the mains doors at the back, with clear air beneath their feet.

At which point, they were gently lowered to the ground.

Once again, I apologise for the nature of this demonstration. I normally prefer to use my powers, slowly returning as they are, for the benefit of the needy. I would ask you to remain where you are please.

I have chosen to speak to you all for a number of reasons, the first of which is an apology, my third today. I deeply wish to apologise to you all for my absence for such a very long time.

When I explain this absence and other matters, you will likely have many questions to ask of me. I will try to answer some questions now, but time is limited. So I request of you, my creatures, to arrange another opportunity for me to talk to a mass audience.

A few minutes had elapsed of the scheduled ten minutes. The BBC, the organisers of the summit and the audience Worldwide desperately wanted this meeting with the Lord to be allowed to take its natural course, even if this took hours.

But God was the only voice that had spoken – not one person had uttered a single word. They were humbled by His presence. Most deeply in awe were of course the religious leaders, all to be found knelt in various supine postures of subservience on the floor.

Intermingled with this awe was, however, some discomfort. He had rather a lot to explain by describing himself as both God and Allah. For now, their subservience and sheer curiosity for more kept all from speaking.

But one voice broke the silence. It was Rowan, compelled in his role as event organiser as it were, to ask God if He was able to stay a while longer in order to ask questions.

"As your humble servant" he started, "I would like to request your presence just a little longer in order that we may ask questions of you now. To wait for another day would be too painful I fear."

> *Thank you for this request.*
>
> *If the BBC are happy to continue broadcasting, I am happy to continue beyond the scheduled time.*

A spokesman for the BBC swiftly gave the nod, and God continued.

> *There are dark forces that you know mostly as the devil or*

Satan. I have always fought these forces, but for the last few millennia, they have held me captive. I cannot describe in your terms this captivity, but suffice to say, it has left me with precious little energy or time to care for you, my creatures. I believe that I am now mostly free from the grip of these satanic forces, and able once again to turn my attention to you all. I have started attending to various matters, some small, some large, but there is much more for me to do. So I ask of you to have patience with me.

I feel that I have said all that I need to say for now, and invite questions. I will limit this to one question per person from each of the key dignitaries in attendance here. I do so for economy of time, and ask that you do not feel that I am overtly biased towards people in a position of power. I select them for the likely succinctness and appropriateness of their questioning.

The World questions

The quiet that had overtaken the building was broken now by fervent chatter. The G8 delegates walked from the rear of the room to join the religious leaders. They briefly huddled in a group before Rowan broke away to speak to the audience and God.

"We humbly thank you for allowing us this time for questions. We will present our questions in no particular order, and hope that you can bear with us, for any clumsiness in the words we use, and the questions we ask" Rowan said.

"Since I am already speaking, I will be the first to ask a question of you, my Lord."

"We all believed that you, God, were all powerful. Yet you talk of a contest with Satan. Are there limits to your power?"

And God replied :

> *Thank you for your question. I am afraid that in my absence over centuries now, what has been recorded about me has become somewhat distorted and misconstrued. When faced with a larger than life power, it is a human tendency to exaggerate. My powers are difficult to describe in human terms, but they are very much finite.*

After Rowan thanked God for his answer, the Islamic representative was next to speak.

"You refer to yourself as both God and Allah. We Muslims are brought up to believe that there is only one Allah. That the God of Christianity is a fabrication. The Christian faith believes that

Jesus is your son, and somehow he is you also. We believe that Jesus was a messenger for your word, but that Allah is a single God. Can you please enlighten me?" he asked.

> *You ask a very good question. However I answer, even though I tell the truth, will cause deep upset to many millions of people who hold misinformed views.*
>
> *It is sad to me, now that I am able to turn my attention back to the planet and all the life that tries to thrive but often struggles to live upon it, that the centuries of my absence has driven them into contradictory and opposing directions.*
>
> *But I must answer truthfully and must then deal with the aftermath. I ask of you to hold no grievance against your fellow man, woman or child, regardless of the errors in their thinking. They were in no position to be enlightened until now, and I make a fourth apology – that it has taken so long for me to speak to you as I do now.*
>
> *Jesus was indeed a messenger. He was a fine man, and I was able to help him promote a respectful life by enabling him to carry out healings and such like.*
>
> *He was not my son however, for I am but one entity. Call me God, Allah, or any of the other names you bestow upon me. I am just me.*

Gasps of surprise, shock and elation permeated the building. But these outbursts were swiftly dampened by the Islamic spokesman.

"Thank you, Allah, for your answer. Whilst Muslims will of course feel vindicated by what you say, I can sense that there is a deeper meaning to what you are telling us which transcends any new sense of superiority that the supporters of the Islamic faith might now feel over other faiths, and indeed over the atheists and agnostics of the world."

"I am allowed only one question, but I would like to take this opportunity to make one statement to the collected audience ...

You are in the presence of Allah. He is real insofar as we can hear his voice and sense his power. And I ask of the world to take this opportunity to forget our differences and join together as one in harmony. Our God is more real than ever, and will take us into a new world order. We miss this opportunity at our peril."

As he finished, his final words were drowned in a cascade of cheers and clapping hands, everyone to a man standing in unified appreciation.

The next to ask a question was the Japanese delegate.

"This is not easy for me, you understand" he started, speaking via an interpreter.

"In common with many Japanese, I am an atheist, and now find myself talking with God. I have experienced enough today to have lost any doubt that you are who you say you are. But to come to terms with this is a struggle of great magnitude for me."

"There are many important questions that I should ask of you, a being that until this afternoon I categorically felt did not exist. But I am too humbled and also obliged to ask but one question. You are claimed to be perfect. Now that you are regaining your powers, will you make the world perfect?" he asked.

I thank you for your courage in facing me. I hope to show you in the coming years that I am not a force to fear. In answer to your question, just as I am not all powerful, I am not perfect. Those that describe me thus do so without much depth of thought.

If they were to follow through with their thinking, they would realise that the concept is meaningless to ascribe to an entity such as myself, just as it is to ascribe to many other things.

Ask a car maker to make the most perfect car in the world, and they will hesitate. They will ask if it should be powerful, or fast, or efficient, or attractive. What is perfect for one person is not so for another. Perfection is sensed in a thing, not an invariant attribute of that thing. When dealing with humans, compromise permeates everything. It is a way of life. If I were to be perfectly fair with everyone on the planet, then I would treat no one differently. Would you all want to be the same? If I made one person tall and another short, then this would give some advantages to the taller person in some situations, and advantages to the short person in other situations.

Life is to be lived for what it is. I would like you to explore the riches that life can offer, but it will remain imperfect. This very imperfection is a source of many of the joys of life – a good day is so much sweeter when it has followed a bad day.

This response solicited a follow up question by the German delegate.

"Like my Japanese colleague, until today, I was not convinced of the existence of God. I like to think that I was fairer of mind in my agnostic stance, but it was probably more the case that I was hedging my bets."

"The single thing that turned me away from religions was the contradiction between claims that you are all loving, all compassionate and all powerful, and yet are able to allow such suffering to permeate the lives of so many people."

"Being held hostage, as it were, by Satan, I can understand why such suffering might have persisted. And I have indeed noticed in the last few weeks some strange changes in the world. Amongst other unusual events, an interim report from a seismology conference in Japan claims that tectonic plate collision activity has all but ceased. I strongly believe that you were responsible for this sudden change. The report even speculated this, although at the time I dismissed this as a foolish whim."

"My question to you is this. Do you plan to remove all suffering from the world?" he asked of the Lord.

And the Lord replied :

You ask a very good question. Whilst held hostage, as you

say, I was often aware of the degree of suffering that beset the world and its people and animals. And yes, I do of course care equally for all of my creatures.

It grieved me deeply that I was witness to so much pain and suffering in the world, whilst being incapable of doing enough about it. My plan now is to carry out a Balancing Act – to redress the greater imbalances in the world.

Suffering has its rightful place in the world – it is right that you have toothache when your tooth needs repairing because you ate too much sweet food. But this toothache will no longer keep you awake at night. And those that eat sensibly – those that have their own lives in balance – will not suffer thus. I will ensure such fairness, as I abhor unnecessary pain and suffering.

However, they are still a part of the fabric of life. But if there is too much, then life is pushed to one side. If your life is so heavily impacted by suffering, then you are not living a full life.

I want to give you equality – so that each of you can have a broadly equal capacity to live a full life. Every life itself will be different, but I will remove arbitrary and pointless suffering, from insomnia to cancer. However, this subject is too large to discuss fully now.

Can I please have the next question?

The Baha'I faith representative was next ...

"With the advent of the Internet, there is a huge clash of theist and non theist argument concerning the origin of life on Earth. The atheists and scientists declare evolution as the answer to all such questions, furnished as it is with a wealth of evidence. The theists counter argue with Intelligent Design. Can you please enlighten us all?" he asked.

God answered this somewhat tricky question :

I am supposed to have created all life on the planet. This, I assure you, is both true and false. Evolution theory describes well the changes in each species on earth as time passes. But it describes change, not instigation. The creation of life from non life in the first place is called Abiogenesis. This is where I was involved. I live outside of the domain of the Earth much as a human resides outside of a fish tank.

When I created the first simple organisms, I was not aware that life would evolve into such complex creatures as humans. But you are my ultimate creation, and I care for you, much as a good Mother cares for her son whether he grows up to be good or bad.

I have the power to manipulate matter on Earth in ways that you would not understand. But life is fragile, and the joy of the diversity of your lives becomes the joy of my life. Likewise, when you suffer, I suffer.

If you want to ascribe the creation of life as it is now to anyone, you should give the credit to cells. You were created by cell division and specialisation. I claim credit for creating the first simple uni-cellular and simple multi-cellular organisms, and steering subsequent evolution.

As my powers were being weakened by those satanic forces, the interplay of life-forms took many bad paths that I could no longer fix.
Now I am able to start remedying the problems that lead to so much suffering in the world.

And so the questions continued. God patiently explained that killing in the name of God, by whatever name, was fundamentally unsociable, and thereby not desirable.

He explained that He was only capable of part of this great Balancing Act. He explained that the growing divide between the very rich and very poor was of no real health or happiness benefit for the rich or of course for the poor – the rich were way richer than they needed to be, rarely gaining from their excesses, and often suffering from the imbalance they it created in their lives.

God fielded questions for a further two hours, after which he concluded this extraordinary programme :

I will leave you now, for I have much to do elsewhere.

I thank you for listening to me, and for your questions.

I look forward to a more harmonious world as the years pass.

Please go in peace.

Printed in Poland
by Amazon Fulfillment
Poland Sp. z o.o., Wrocław